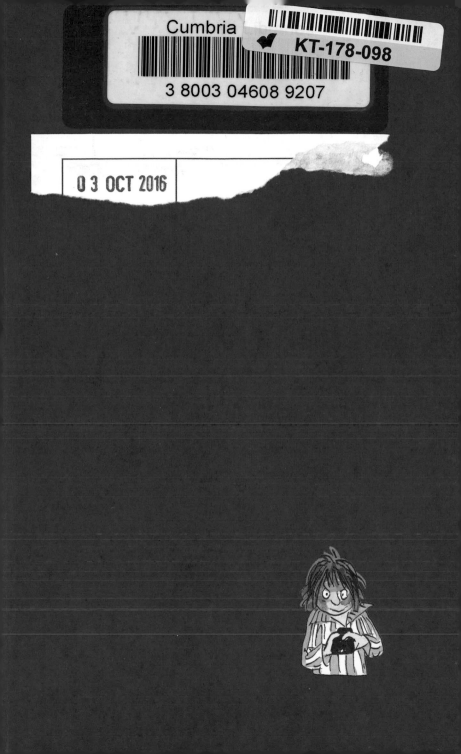

HORRiD HENRY
and the
Comfy Black Chair

HORRID HENRY
and the
Comfy Black Chair

Francesca Simon
Illustrated by Tony Ross

Orion
Children's Books

Horrid Henry and the Comfy Black Chair originally appeared in
Horrid Henry's Haunted House,
first published in
Great Britain in 1999
by Orion Children's Books
This edition published in Great Britain in 2015
by Orion Children's Books, an imprint of Hachette's
Children's Group, a division of Hodder and Stoughton Limited
Orion House
5 Upper St Martin's Lane
London WC2H 9EA
An Hachette UK company

1 3 5 7 9 10 8 6 4 2

ISBN 978 1 4440 0882 1

A catalogue record for this book is available from the British Library.

Printed in China

www.orionbooks.co.uk
www.horridhenry.co.uk

For Alicia and David Simon,
and for Joel and Donna Simon,
the original proud owners
of the comfy black chair.

For a complete list of the **Horrid Henry**
books available, look at the back of the book.
Or visit
www.horridhenry.co.uk
or
www.orionbooks.co.uk

Contents

Chapter 1

Ah, Saturday! Best day of the week, thought Horrid Henry, flinging off the covers and leaping out of bed.

No school! No homework!
A day of TV heaven!

Mum and Dad liked sleeping in on a
Saturday. So long as Henry and Peter
were quiet they could watch TV until
Mum and Dad woke up.

Horrid Henry could picture it now.
He would stretch out in the comfy
black chair, grab the remote control,
and switch on the TV. All his favourite
shows were on today: *Rapper Zapper*,
Mutant Max, and *Gross-Out*.
If he hurried he would be just
in time for *Rapper Zapper*.

He thudded down the stairs and
flung open the sitting room door.

A horrible sight met his eyes.

There, stretched out on the comfy
black chair and clutching the remote
control, was his younger brother,
Perfect Peter.

Henry gasped. How could this be?
Henry always got downstairs first.
The TV was already on. But it was
not switched to *Rapper Zapper*.

A terrible tinkly tune trickled out
of the TV. Oh no! It was the world's
most boring show, *Daffy and her
Dancing Daisies*.

"Switch the channel!" ordered Horrid Henry. "*Rapper Zapper*'s on."

"That's a horrid, nasty programme," said Perfect Peter, shuddering. He held tight to the remote.

"I said switch the channel!" hissed Henry.

"I won't!" said Peter. "You know
the rules. The first one downstairs
gets to sit in the comfy black chair
and decides what to watch.
And I want to watch *Daffy*."

Henry could hardly believe his ears.
Perfect Peter was . . . refusing to obey
an order?

"NO!" screamed Henry.
"I hate that show. I want to watch
Rapper Zapper!"

"Well, I want to watch *Daffy*,"
said Perfect Peter.

"But that's a baby show," said Henry.

"Dance, my daisies, dance!"
squealed the revolting Daffy.

"La, la la la la!" trilled the Daisies.

"La, la la la la!" sang Peter.

"Baby, baby!" taunted Henry. If only he could get Peter to run upstairs crying then *he* could get the chair.

"Peter is a baby, Peter is a baby!" jeered Henry.

Peter kept his eyes glued to the screen.

Horrid Henry could stand it no
longer. He pounced on Peter,
snatched the remote, and pushed
Peter onto the floor. He was *Rapper
Zapper* liquidating a pesky android.

"AAAAAH!" screamed Perfect Peter.
"Muummm!"

Horrid Henry leaped into the comfy black chair and switched channels.

"Grrrrrrr!" growled Rapper Zapper, blasting a baddie.

"Don't be horrid, Henry!"

shouted Mum, storming
through the door.

"Go to your room!"

"Noooo!"

wailed Henry. "Peter started it!"

"NOW!" screamed Mum.

"La, la la la la!" trilled the Daisies.

Chapter 2

BUZZZZZZZZ.

Horrid Henry switched off the alarm.
It was six a.m. the following Saturday.

Henry was taking no chances.
Even if he had to grit his teeth
and watch *Rise and Shine* before
Gross-Out started it was worth it.
And he'd seen the coming attractions
for today's *Gross-Out*: who could
eat the most cherry pie in five
minutes while blasting the other
contestants with a goo-shooter.

Henry couldn't wait.

There was no sound from Peter's room. Ha, ha, thought Henry. He'll have to sit on the lumpy sofa and watch what *I* want to watch.

Horrid Henry skipped into
the sitting room.

And stopped.

"Remember, children, always eat with a knife and fork!" beamed a cheerful presenter. It was *Manners with Maggie*. There was Perfect Peter in his slippers and dressing gown, stretched out on the comfy black chair. Horrid Henry felt sick.

Another Saturday ruined! He had to watch *Gross-Out*! He just had to.

Horrid Henry was just about to push
Peter off the chair when he stopped.
Suddenly he had a brilliant idea.

"Peter! Mum and Dad want to see
you. They said it's urgent!"

Perfect Peter leaped off the comfy
black chair and dashed upstairs.

Tee hee, thought Horrid Henry.

ZAP!

"Welcome to *GROSS-OUT*!"
shrieked the presenter,
Marvin the Maniac. "Boy, will you
all be feeling sick today! It's
GROSS!

GROSS!

GROSS!"

"Yeah!" said Horrid Henry.
This was great!

Perfect Peter reappeared.
"They didn't want me," said Peter.
"And they're cross because I woke
them up."

"They told me they did," said Henry,
eyes glued to the screen.

Peter stood still.
"Please give me the chair back,
Henry."

Henry didn't answer.
"I had it first," said Peter.

"Shut up, I'm trying to watch,"
said Henry.

"Ewwwwww, gross!"
screamed the TV audience.

"I was watching *Manners with Maggie,*"
said Peter. "She's showing how to eat
soup without slurping."

"Tough," said Henry.
"Oh, gross!" he chortled,
pointing at the screen.

Peter hid his eyes.
"Muuuuummmmmmmm!" shouted
Peter. "Henry's being mean to me!"

Mum appeared in the doorway.
She looked furious.
"Henry, go to your room!" shouted
Mum. "We were trying to sleep.
Is it too much to ask to be left in
peace one morning a week?"

"But Peter—"

Mum pointed to the door.
"Out!" said Mum.

"It's not fair!" howled Henry,
stomping off.

ZAP!

"And now Kate, our guest manners expert, will demonstrate the proper way to butter toast."

Henry slammed the door behind him
as hard as he could. Peter had got
the comfy black chair for the very
last time.

Chapter 3

BUZZZZZZ.

Horrid Henry switched off the alarm. It was two a.m. the *following* Saturday. The *Gross-Out* Championships were on in the morning.

He grabbed his pillow and duvet
and sneaked out of the room.
He was taking no chances. Tonight he
would *sleep* in the comfy black chair.
After all, Mum and Dad had never
said how *early* he could get up.

Henry tiptoed out of his room
into the hall.
All quiet in Peter's room.
All quiet in Mum and Dad's.

Henry crept down the stairs and carefully opened the sitting room door. The room was pitch black. Better not turn on the light, thought Henry.

He felt his way along the wall until his fingers touched the back of the comfy black chair. He felt around the top. Ah, there was the remote. He'd sleep with that under his pillow, just to be safe.

Henry flung himself onto the chair
and landed on something lumpy.

"AHHHHHHHHH!"
screamed Henry.

"AHHHHHHHHH!"
screamed the Lump.

"HELP!"
screamed Henry and the Lump.

Feet pounded down the stairs.
"What's going on down there?"
shouted Dad, switching on the light.

Henry blinked.

"Henry jumped on my head!"
snivelled a familiar voice beneath him.

"Henry, what are you doing?"
said Dad. "It's two o'clock in
the morning!"

Henry's brain whirled.
"I thought I heard a burglar so
I crept down to keep watch."

"Henry's lying!" said Peter, sitting up. "He came down because he wanted the comfy black chair."

"Liar!" said Henry. "And what were *you* doing down here?"

"I couldn't sleep and I didn't want to wake you, Dad," said Peter. "So I came down as quietly as I could to get a drink of water. Then I felt sleepy and lay down for a moment. I'm very sorry, Dad, it will never happen again."

"All right," said Dad, stifling a yawn.
"From now on, you are not to
come down here before seven a.m.
or there will be no TV for a week!
Is that clear?"

"Yes, Dad," said Peter.

"Yeah," muttered Henry.
He glared at Perfect Peter.

Perfect Peter glared at Horrid Henry.
Then they both went upstairs to their
bedrooms and closed the doors.
"Goodnight!" called Henry cheerfully.
"My, I'm sleepy."

Chapter 4

But Henry did not go to bed.
He needed to think.
He *could* wait until everyone was
asleep and sneak back down. But
what if he got caught? No TV for
a week would be unbearable.

But what if he missed the *Gross-Out*
Championships? And never found out
if Tank Thomas or Tapioca Tina
won the day? Henry shuddered.
There had to be a better way.
Ahh! He had it!

He would set his clock ahead and
make sure he was first down. Brilliant!
Gross-Out here I come, he thought.

But wait.

What if Peter had the *same* brilliant idea? That would spoil everything. Henry had to double-check.

Henry opened his bedroom door.
The coast was clear. He tiptoed out
and sneaked into Peter's room.
There was Peter, sound asleep.
And there was his clock.
Peter hadn't changed the time.
Phew.

And then Henry had a truly wicked idea. It was so evil, and so horrid, that for a moment even he hesitated.

But hadn't Peter been horrible and selfish, stopping Henry watching his favourite shows? He certainly had. And wouldn't it be great if Peter got into trouble, just for once?

Perfect Peter rolled over. "La, la la la la," he warbled in his sleep.

That did it. Horrid Henry moved
Peter's clock an hour ahead.
Then Henry sneaked downstairs
and turned up the TV's volume
as loud as it would go.

Finally, he opened Mum and Dad's
door and crept back to bed.

Chapter 5

"It's Grow and Show!
The vegetable show
for tinies!
Just look at all these
lovely vegetables!"

The terrible noise boomed through
the house, blasting Henry out of bed.
"HENRY!" bellowed Dad.
"Come here this instant!"

Henry sauntered into his parents'
bedroom. "What is it?"
he asked, yawning loudly.

Mum and Dad looked confused.
"Wasn't that you watching TV
downstairs?"

"No," said Henry, stretching.
"I was asleep."

Mum looked at Dad.
Dad looked at Mum.

"You mean *Peter* is downstairs
watching TV at six a.m.?"
Henry shrugged.
"Send Peter up here this minute!"
said Dad.

For once Henry did not need to be
asked twice. He ran downstairs and
burst into the sitting room.

"I grew carrots!"
"I grew string beans!"

"Peter! Mum and Dad want to see
you right away!" said Henry.

Peter didn't look away from
Grow and Show.
"PETER! Dad asked me
to send you up!"

"You're just trying to trick me,"
said Peter.

"You'd better go or you'll be in big trouble," said Henry.

"Fool me once, shame on you. Fool me twice, shame on me," said Peter. "I'm not moving."

"Now, just look at all these
beautiful tomatoes Timmy's grown,"
squealed the TV.

"Wow," said Peter.

"Don't say I didn't warn you,"
said Henry.

"Peter!" bellowed Dad. "No TV for a month! Come here this minute!"

Perfect Peter burst into tears. He jumped from the chair and crept out of the room.

Horrid Henry sauntered over to
the comfy black chair and stretched
out. He picked up the remote and
switched channels.

ZAP!

Rapper Zapper stormed into
the spaceship and pulverized some
alien slime.

"Way to go, Rapper Zapper!"
shrieked Horrid Henry.
Soon *Gross-Out* would be on.
Wasn't life sweet?

What are you going to read next?

Have more adventures with Horrid Henry,

or save the day with Anthony Ant!

Become a superhero with Monstar,

float off to sea with Algy,

or have your very own Pirates' Picnic.

Grow carrots with

Lottie and Dottie,

make magic with The Witch Dog,

and cast a spell with

The Three Little Magicians.

Enjoy all the Early Readers.

HORRID HENRY BOOKS

Colour Books
Horrid Henry's Big Bad Book
Horrid Henry's Wicked Ways
Horrid Henry's Evil Enemies
Horrid Henry Rules the World
Horrid Henry's House of Horrors
Horrid Henry's Dreadful Deeds
Horrid Henry Shows Who's Boss
Horrid Henry's A-Z of Everything Horrid
Horrid Henry Fearsome Four
Horrid Henry's Royal Riot
Horrid Henry's Tricky Tricks

Joke Books
Horrid Henry's Joke Book
Horrid Henry's Jolly Joke Book
Horrid Henry's Mighty Joke Book
Horrid Henry versus Moody Margaret
Horrid Henry's Hilariously Horrid Joke Book
Horrid Henry's Purple Hand Gang Joke Book
Horrid Henry's All Time Favourite Joke Book

Activity Books
Horrid Henry's Brainbusters
Horrid Henry's Headscratchers
Horrid Henry's Mindbenders
Horrid Henry's Colouring Book
Horrid Henry's Puzzle Book
Horrid Henry's Sticker Book
Horrid Henry's Classroom Chaos
Horrid Henry's Holiday Havoc
Horrid Henry's Runs Riot
Horrid Henry's Annual 2015
Horrid Henry's Crazy Crosswords
Horrid Henry's Mad Mazes
Horrid Henry's Wicked Wordsearches

Fact Books
Horrid Henry's Ghosts
Horrid Henry's Dinosaurs
Horrid Henry's Sports
Horrid Henry's Food
Horrid Henry's Kings and Queens
Horrid Henry's Bugs
Horrid Henry's Animals
Horrid Henry's Ghosts
Horrid Henry's Crazy Creatures
Horrid Henry's World Records

the
orion star

Sign up for **the orion star** newsletter
for all the latest children's book news,
plus activity sheets, exclusive competitions,
author interviews, pre-publication extracts
and more.

www.orionbooks.co.uk/newsletters

Follow @the_orionstar on **twitter**.

Orion
Children's Books